**4** What is a Bird?

**8** Types of Birds

**10** Birds of Prey

**14** Seabirds

**18** Plant Eaters

**22** Feet, Beaks and Food

**23** Glossary and Index

# What is a Bird?

## A bird is an animal with a backbone, wings and feathers.

emu

All birds have wings, and most birds can fly. The wings have light, hollow bones that help birds fly.

All birds have feathers. Feathers help birds to fly. They also keep birds warm and dry.

Not all birds can fly. Penguins can't fly but they are good at swimming. Emus can't fly but they can run very quickly.

All birds lay eggs. Most birds build nests for their eggs. The eggs need to be kept warm until they hatch. Some birds feed and care for their baby birds, or chicks, as they grow.

A bird uses its wings and feathers to fly.

wing

beak

claws

5

# Life Cycle of a Bird

How a bird grows from an egg to an adult.

**1** Birds lay their eggs in a nest. Parent birds warm the eggs with their bodies.

**2** When the eggs hatch, the chicks are helpless.

**3** The parents feed and care for the chicks.

**4** The chicks grow up and learn how to fly. The young birds now have to find their own food.

7

# Types of Birds

There are many different types of birds. There are more than 9 000 species. They live all over the world.

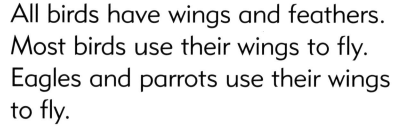

All birds have wings and feathers. Most birds use their wings to fly. Eagles and parrots use their wings to fly.

Penguins can't fly. They use their wings like flippers when they swim.

Birds eat different things. Some birds eat small animals or insects. Others eat food from plants.

**Birds of prey**, such as eagles and owls, have sharp **beaks** to eat animals. Birds of the sea eat fish. Parrots have strong beaks to break open seeds.

Eagles perch or soar while looking for prey.

Macaws live in rainforests.

Penguins are seabirds.

Birds of prey hunt and
eat animals.

There are many different birds of prey. Eagles, hawks, owls and vultures are all birds of prey. They live in many parts of the world.

Birds of prey have strong, sharp claws or **talons**. They use them to catch and carry their food.

Birds of prey have sharp, hooked beaks. They use them to tear up their food.

Birds of prey have big, strong wings. These help them to fly and hunt for hours at a time.

great horned owl

Eagles tear meat from their prey with their sharp beaks.

Vultures have big, strong wings.

Hawks have keen eyesight and sharp beaks.

11

# Eagles

Eagles are birds of prey. Birds of prey hunt and eat animals.

Eagles have big, strong wings. These help them to fly very high and fast. Eagles can glide on air currents and watch for **prey**.

Eagles can dive on their prey from great heights. They eat rats, rabbits, snakes, lizards and other birds. Some eagles also eat fish.

sharp, hooked beak

big, strong wings

sharp talons

Eagles build nests in trees.

**FASTEST!**

The peregrine falcon is the fastest animal on earth.

| Bird | Number of species |
|---|---|
| eagles | 224 |
| falcons | 62 |
| owls | 135 |

Eagles have strong, stiff wing feathers that spread out like fingers.

# Seabirds

## Seabirds depend on the sea for their food.

Many birds can swim or dive to catch fish. Penguins and pelicans live near the water and feed on fish.

Seabirds have webbed feet. This helps them to swim.

Seabirds have an oil gland near their tails. Using their beaks they cover their feathers with oil. Oily feathers keep seabirds warm and dry.

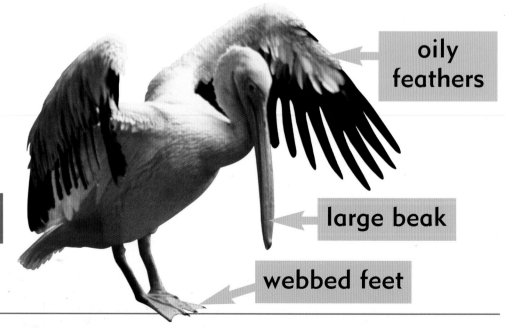

pelican

oily feathers

large beak

webbed feet

Rockhopper penguins travel together for safety.

Seagulls can drink salt water.

Puffins can fly. They also swim under water.

15

## GO FACTS

### LONGEST!

Pelicans have the longest beak of any bird.

| Bird | Number of species |
| --- | --- |
| gulls | 95 |
| penguins | 16 |
| pelicans | 7 |

# Penguins

Penguins are seabirds. Seabirds depend on the sea for their food.

Penguins cannot fly but they are very good swimmers. They use their wings like flippers when they swim.

Penguins eat fish. They dive under the water to hunt for fish. They can hold their breath for a long time.

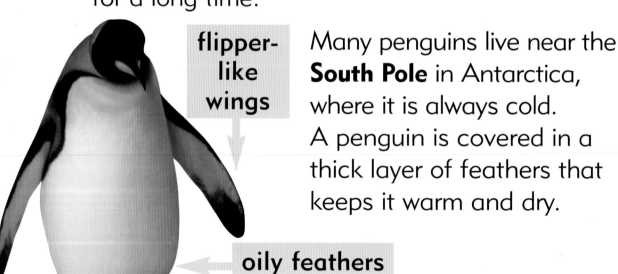

**flipper-like wings**

**oily feathers**

**webbed feet**

Many penguins live near the **South Pole** in Antarctica, where it is always cold. A penguin is covered in a thick layer of feathers that keeps it warm and dry.

Emperor penguins are the largest penguins.

Penguins mate for life.

17

# Plant Eaters

Many birds feed on plants. They eat seeds and fruit or drink nectar.

Some seed eaters have sharp, strong beaks. They use them to crack seeds open. Other seed eaters swallow seeds whole.

Fruit eaters have large, hooked beaks. They use them to tear open fruit.

**Nectar**-eating birds, such as hummingbirds, have long, thin beaks. They use their beaks to suck nectar from flowers.

toucan

Parrots eat seeds and fruit.

This tufted titmouse is carrying an acorn.

Hummingbirds can beat their wings up to 80 times per second.

| Bird | Number of species |
|------|-------------------|
| hummingbirds | 315 |
| parrots | 330 |
| pigeons | 300 |

A hummingbird can fly backwards and upside down.

# Parrots

Parrots are birds that eat plants. They eat fruit and seeds.

small wings

strong, hooked beak

claws

Parrots live in trees. Most have small wings so they can easily fly through thick forest trees. They build nests in the hollows of trees.

Parrots have strong, hooked beaks. They use their beaks to crack open seeds and to eat fruit.

Parrots are **perching** birds. They have claws that can wrap around a branch. They can also use their claws to pick up and hold their food.

The powerful beak of a macaw is sometimes used to help it climb trees.

# Feet, Beaks and Food

| | Feet | Beak | Food |
|---|---|---|---|
| **eagle** | strong talons | | small animals, fish |
| **hawk** | strong talons | | small animals |
| **penguin** | webbed feet | | fish |
| **pelican** | webbed feet | | fish |
| **parrot** | perching claws | | fruit and seeds |
| **macaw** | perching claws | | fruit and seeds |

# Glossary

| | |
|---|---|
| backbone | the spine |
| beak | the hard mouth part of a bird |
| bird of prey | a bird that hunts animals |
| nectar | a sweet liquid from flowers |
| perching | sitting with claws wrapped around a branch |
| prey | an animal that is hunted as food |
| South Pole | the southernmost place on Earth |
| species | animals that can breed together |
| talons | sharp, hooked claws |

 # Index

bird of prey  8, 10, 12

chick  4, 6

claws  10, 12, 20, 22

eagle  8, 10, 12, 22

eggs  4, 6

hawk  10, 22

macaw  22

nests  4, 20

owl  8, 10

pelican  14, 22

seabirds  14, 16

vulture  10

webbed feet  14, 16, 22